MAKING THE MOOSE OUT OF LIFE

To Abbey, Quinn, Dexter and Nico

First paperback edition 2015

Text and illustrations © 2010 Nicholas Oldland

Kids Can Press gratefully acknowledges the financial support of the Government of Ontario, through Ontario Creates; the Ontario Arts Council; the Canada Council for the Arts; and the Government of Canada for our publishing activity.

Published in Canada and the U.S. by Kids Can Press Ltd.
25 Dockside Drive, Toronto, ON M5A 0B5

Kids Can Press is a Corus Entertainment Inc. company

www.kidscanpress.com

The artwork in this book was rendered in Photoshop.
The text is set in Animated Gothic.

Edited by Yvette Ghione
Designed by Marie Bartholomew

Printed and bound in Malaysia in 6/2019 by Tien Wah Press (Pte.) Ltd.

CM 10 20 19 18 17 16 15 14 13 12
CM PA 15 0 9 8 7 6 5

Library and Archives Canada Cataloguing in Publication

Oldland, Nicholas, 1972–, author, illustrator
Making the moose out of life / Nicholas Oldland.

(Life in the wild)
ISBN 978-1-55453-580-4 (bound)   ISBN 978-1-55453-627-6 (pbk.)

I. Moose — Juvenile fiction. I. Title. II. Series.

PS8629.L46M36 2015   jC813'.6   C2014-908268-1

MAKING THE MOOSE OUT OF LIFE

Nicholas Oldland

Kids Can Press

There once was a moose who lived in the wild
but didn't act wild at all.

When it rained, his friends would go puddle jumping. Not this moose. Too wet.

When the wind blew, his friends would go kite flying. Not this moose. Too windy.

When it snowed, his friends would go skiing. Not this moose. Too cold.

But every now and then, the moose got the feeling he was missing out on something.

What could it be?

OMMM

The moose tried meditating ...

Searching the Internet ...

Looking into a crystal ball ...

Praying to the Moose above ...

And scanning the night sky.

But the moose didn't find a thing.

One sunny day, the moose was struck with a thought: He needed to take life by the antlers if he was going to find that something missing. In the same instant he noticed the sailboat at the water's edge, its sail gently flapping in the breeze. The moose was inspired.

With his friends looking on, the moose set sail.

But what started as a gentle breeze ...

Turned into a strong wind ...

And soon became a raging storm.

The moose battled the storm till he could fight no more.

In the morning, the moose woke up scared and alone on a deserted island.

Normally this moose would have curled into a ball and cried. But that day he took a deep breath and got to work.

The moose located a source of fresh water ...

Gathered wood and made a signal fire ...

Built a shelter ...

Climbed for coconuts ...

Learned to spear fish ...

And met a tortoise named Tuesday.

Over the following days and weeks, the moose faced
many challenges and thought of home often. But with
Tuesday by his side, he made the most of island life.

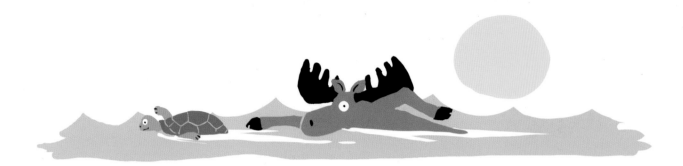

When it was hot, they went swimming.

When the waves were big,
they surfed.

When it was cold, they roasted
coconuts by the fire.

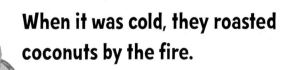

Life was pretty good.

Then, just as the moose was about to pour Tuesday another coconut smoothie one evening, a ship appeared on the horizon. Quickly they threw more wood on the fire to get the crew's attention.

When the ship came to the moose's rescue, the two friends said their good-byes, promised to write and made plans to get together over the holidays.

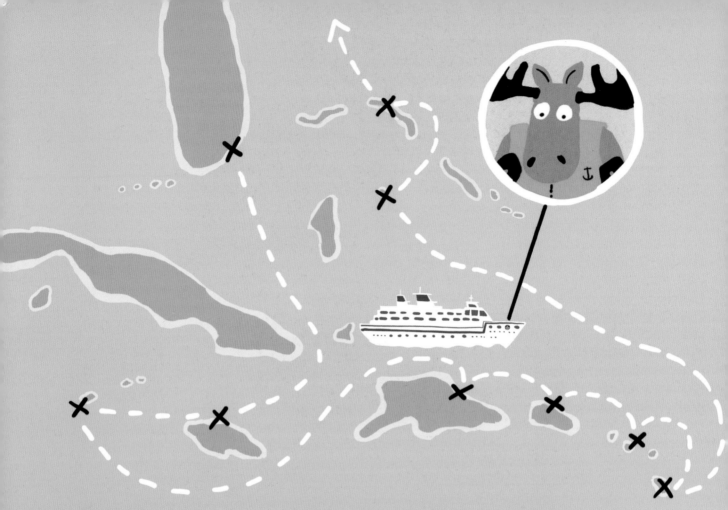

The moose had been rescued on day three of a two-week Caribbean cruise. At first he was nervous about being back at sea. But when the moose finally left his cabin, it didn't take him long to embrace the cruise ship lifestyle.

He enjoyed all-day buffets ...

Shuffleboard on the lido deck ...

And all-night card games.

When the moose finally arrived home, his friends could hardly believe their eyes. The beaver and the bear thought they had lost their friend forever. They gave him a big welcome home hug. And when the once mild-mannered moose said, "Let's go cliff jumping!" his friends were overjoyed.

Dear Tuesday,

I feel like a new moose.
I am always doing
something fun and exciting.
Can't wait for the holidays.
I miss you. Have you ever
been to Africa?

Love, Moose